"Who knows what a synonym is?" Miss Simms asked.

I shouted out, "They're those sticky things that taste good."

"No, those are cinnamon buns," she laughed.

"A synonym is a word that means the same thing as another word like buddy, friend, pal."

"Who can tell me what a thesaurus is?" Miss Simms asked.

I hollered again, "It's a giant, green monster."

She chuckled. "No, that's a tyrannosaurus, Boris. A thesaurus is a big book where all of the synonyms live."

I had never seen such a big book before.
It was filled with
hundreds,
no, thousands,
maybe millions of words.

THESAURUS

The
**BIG,
GIANT,
HUGE
BOOK OF WORDS**

There were too many words to read. Besides, it was almost time for lunch, and my stomach was growling. I just couldn't stop thinking about those cinnamon buns.

That's when it happened. I picked up the thesaurus and devoured each and every word.

I started with the A's and chewed my way through the alphabet. I didn't even stop for a drink of water. **L, M, N, oh my!** I just kept going.

By the time I reached the X, Y, and ZZZ's, I was ready for a nap. I put my head down on the desk, and suddenly, I belted out the world's biggest

When I came home that night, I skipped dinner. I wasn't hungry.
My mom asked if I had eaten something at the library. "Just a thesaurus,"
I replied. My mom said that she didn't remember packing one in my lunch box.

My mom rushed me to the doctor. Never before had the doctor seen such a case. She looked inside my stomach and saw hundreds, no, thousands, maybe millions of words. I explained I never really AIMED, INTENDED, PLANNED to eat a thesaurus. It just sort of DEVELOPED, HAPPENED, OCCURRED.

My mom was afraid that all of these words would make me sick.
But, the doctor told her not to worry.
She said that I just had a mild case of worditis.
"What's that?" my mom asked.

"I'm CHATTY, GABBY, TALKATIVE," I rattled off.

I take it your speech didn't go so well?" she asked.

What speech?" I **MUMBLED, MUTTERED, WHISPERED.** "I ran out of words."

Well, then you've come to the right place," she said. "All of the words in the world are right ere in these books. The secret to remember is that books are for reading, not for eating. very time you read, you discover new words that last a lifetime."

I picked up a book
and started reading.
It was a delicious story.

The **CONCLUSION, END, FINISH**

For my parents, who never ran out of
encouraging, inspiring, motivating words.
Neil Steven Klayman

In loving memory of my parents, who inspired
my creative spirit to fly, rise, soar.
Barry M. Chung

Originally published by Rainbow Bridge Publishing, an imprint of
Carson-Dellosa Publishing, Greensboro, North Carolina, in 2007.
This edition published by Super Senses Productions, LLC,
Los Angeles, California, in 2011.

Boris Ate a Thesaurus™ and all related and associated trademarks are owned
by Cookie Jar Entertainment Inc. and used under license by Super Senses
Productions, LLC. © 2007 by Cookie Jar Entertainment. All rights reserved.

This title was originally cataloged by the Library of Congress as follows:

Klayman, Neil Steven.
  Boris ate a thesaurus / written by Neil Steven Klayman ; illustrated by Barry M. Chung.
     p. cm.
  Summary: A hungry boy learns that books are for reading and not for swallowing after he eats a thesaurus and starts speaking in
synonyms.
   ISBN 978-0-9839774-0-7
  [1. Thesauri--Fiction. 2. English language--Synonyms and antonyms--Fiction. 3. Books and reading--Fiction. 4. Humorous stories.] I.
Chung, Barry M., ill. II. Title.
   PZ7.K678315Bo 2007
   [E]--dc22
                              2007001607

The text for this book was primarily set
in Billy Regular.
The illustrations were rendered digitally.
Project Manager, Jennifer Weaver-Spencer.
Production by Chasity Rice.

Printed in China.